# THOMAS & FRIENDS

™

The Thomas TV Series

# EGMONT

*We bring stories to life*

This edition first published in Great Britain in 2013
by Dean, an imprint of Egmont UK Limited
The Yellow Building, 1 Nicholas Road,
London W11 4AN

Thomas the Tank Engine & Friends™

CREATED BY BRITT ALLCROFT

HiT entertainment

ISBN 978 0 6035 6685 1
51664/1
Printed in China

# THOMAS, PERCY
# AND THE SQUEAK

The engines on the Island of Sodor love the summer. Sometimes, The Fat Controller holds concerts.

One morning the engines were very excited. Alicia Botti, the famous singer, was coming to Sodor to sing at The Fat Controller's concert.

"I'm bound to be chosen to collect her," boasted James. "I'm the brightest and the shiniest engine!"

"Nonsense! I'm the most important!" huffed Gordon.

Thomas wanted to feel important, too. "He might choose me," he said, hopefully.

Percy came along next to Gordon. His face was very grimy.

"Well, one thing's for sure," snorted Gordon. "He won't choose dirty Percy."

"I'm dirty because I work hard," said Percy, proudly. And he wheeshed away.

The next day, The Fat Controller came to decide which engine would collect the singer from the Docks.

He didn't choose Gordon.

And he didn't choose James.

He chose Thomas! "Make sure Annie and Clarabel are squeaky clean," he said.

"Yes, Sir!" said Thomas, excitedly. He felt very important indeed.

Thomas hurried off to be cleaned. He wheeshed up next to Percy. "Move aside," said Thomas. "I'm the important engine today."

"But I need a washdown!" wailed Percy. "My passengers will laugh at me."

"You'll have to wait," huffed Thomas. "Today, I have to be squeaky clean."

"Then I'll have to go without being cleaned," said Percy, unhappily. "I'm a guaranteed connection!" He chuffed away, still very dirty.

Soon Thomas was shiny and squeaky clean. He felt more important than ever.

But as the workers coupled Annie and Clarabel together, they heard a strange noise. A funny sort of squeak.

"What's that?" asked Thomas, anxiously.

His Driver quickly oiled Annie and Clarabel's undercarriage.

"That should take care of the annoying squeak," said the Driver.

On the way to the Docks, Thomas heard the squeak again. He was worried now.

When he arrived, a big liner had brought lots of passengers to the Island of Sodor. Alicia Botti was waiting with The Fat Controller.

Thomas squeaked into the quayside.

The Fat Controller held Clarabel's door open for the famous singer. He was pleased to see Thomas looking so clean and shiny. But as Alicia Botti was boarding the train, she saw a mouse inside the carriage!

"SQUEAK!" said the mouse.

"EEEEK! A mouse!" screamed Alicia Botti. And she screamed and screamed and screamed.

She screamed so loudly and for so long that windows broke all over town. Alicia Botti was very cross indeed.

"I can't possibly travel in coaches full of mice," she said.

The Fat Controller was very embarrassed. Thomas didn't feel important at all.

Just then, Percy returned from his guaranteed connection. He looked grimier than ever.

"Just look at the little green engine," Alicia Botti exclaimed. "So sweet . . . and dirty! Like a proper steam engine!"

The Fat Controller called Percy over at once. Alicia Botti boarded the train and Percy steamed away. He felt very proud.

Later that day, Thomas was waiting at the washdown when Percy chuffed up beside him.

"I'm sorry I was so cheeky," peeped Thomas. "You go first."

"Thanks, Thomas. It's good to be friends again," said Percy. "But where is your mouse?"

"You'll see!" grinned Thomas.

The Fat Controller had made the mouse her very own home in the corner of Tidmouth Sheds. And Thomas named her Alicia.